AF394770

# BIG BRILLIANT WORLD

## AYSHA TENGIZ

BPP

# CONTENTS

North America
South America
PACIFIC OCEAN
ATLANTIC OCEAN
SOUTHERN OCEAN
Antarctica
London
Paris
New York
Barcelona
Mexico City

ARCTIC OCEAN
Amsterdam
Berlin
Budapest
Europe
Africa
Asia
Istanbul
Rome
INDIAN OCEAN
PACIFIC OCEAN
Tokyo
Seoul
Australia
N
S
E
W
SOUTHERN OCEAN

# HELLO!

We're about to embark on a journey to **12 incredible cities** and we want YOU to come along with us. This book is your passport to discover the big, the bold and the brilliant!

Every city holds its own stories – from **Budapest**'s magical baths and **Mexico City**'s vibrant food culture to **Rome**'s ancient wonders and **Seoul**'s futuristic technology. Every stop will bring you one step closer to understanding how diverse and fun our world really is.

Along the way, you'll also learn about the different languages spoken in each city – and even pick up some of your first words in those languages! Want to say "hello" in Spanish? Or ask for tea in Korean? By the end of the book, you'll have a collection of words and phrases from around the world.
So, are you ready to begin your adventure? Pack your bags, flip the page and let's get started!

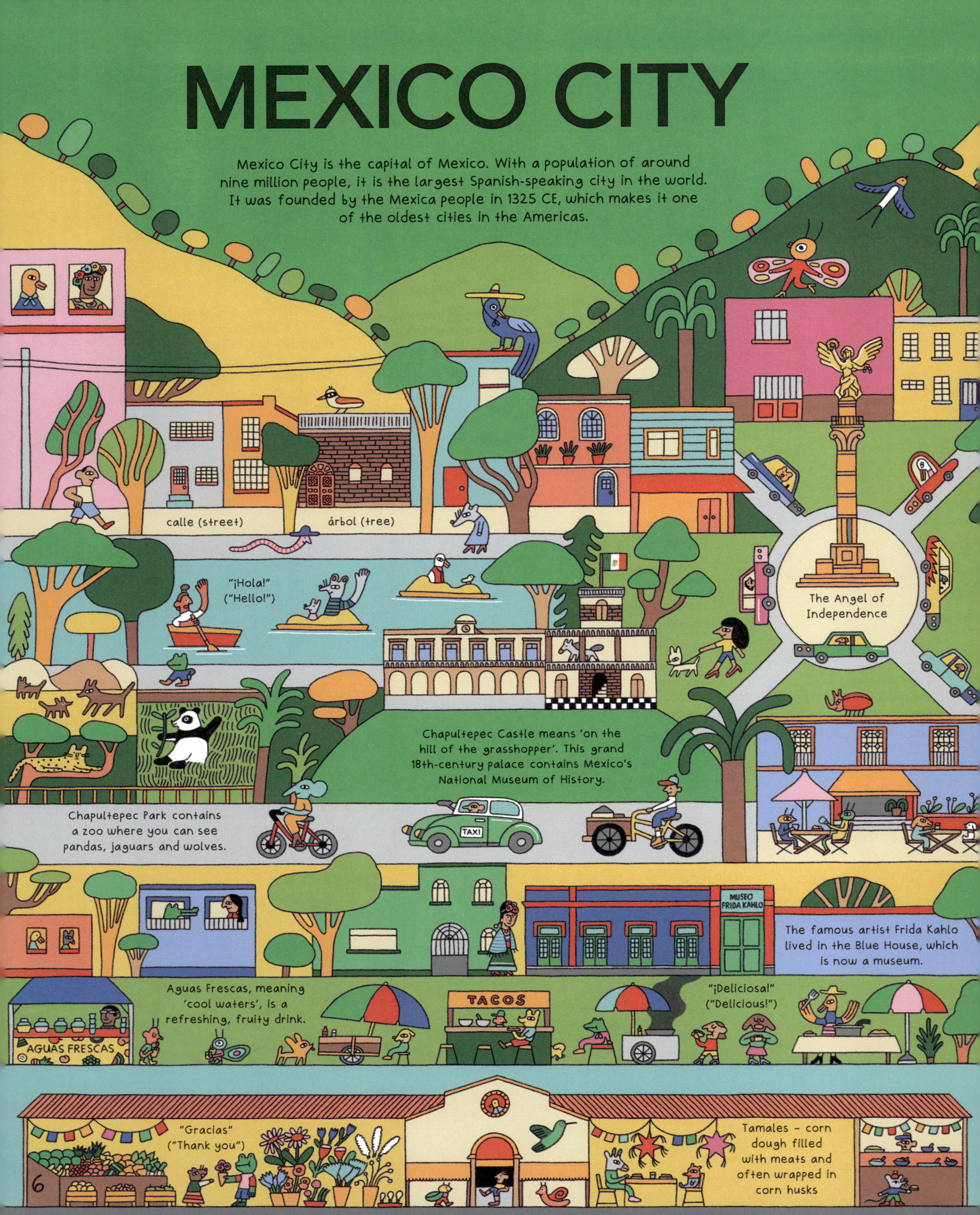

# MEXICO CITY

Mexico City is the capital of Mexico. With a population of around nine million people, it is the largest Spanish-speaking city in the world. It was founded by the Mexica people in 1325 CE, which makes it one of the oldest cities in the Americas.



Chapultepec Castle means 'on the hill of the grasshopper'. This grand 18th-century palace contains Mexico's National Museum of History.

Chapultepec Park contains a zoo where you can see pandas, jaguars and wolves.

The famous artist Frida Kahlo lived in the Blue House, which is now a museum.

Aguas Frescas, meaning 'cool waters', is a refreshing, fruity drink.

Tamales – corn dough filled with meats and often wrapped in corn husks

Mexico City is built on a dried-up lakebed, 2,240 metres above sea level.
"¡No mires abajo!" ("Don't look down!")
"Adiós" ("Goodbye")
The Mexicable is a 14-station cable car transport network.
Plaza Garibaldi
Mariachi bands gather in the Plaza every day to play traditional Mexican folk music.
17:01:18
Metropolitan Cathedral
Monumento a la Revolución
Torre Latinoamericana
El Zócalo is the city's main public square.
Lucha Libre, meaning 'freestyle wrestling', is a popular professional wrestling sport in Mexico.
"¡Eso estuvo de lujo!" ("That was amazing!")
autobús (bus)
The Mexico City Metro has 12 lines and 195 stations. It transports around 5.5 million passengers every day.
The Floating Gardens of Xochimilco are a UNESCO World Culture Heritage Site. The boats here are called 'chalupas'.
Located around 80 kilometres outside of the city sits one of Mexico's most active volcanoes. Its name is Popocatépetl, which means 'Smoking Mountain'.

7

NEW YORK
Sometimes called 'The Big Apple', New York has the most famous skyline in the world. Home to over eight million people, it is the most densely populated city in the USA. Busy, bustling and exciting, New York is a global centre of finance, technology, culture, fashion, media and entertainment.
The High Line is an elevated, scenic park built on a disused stretch of railway line.
Food cart
PIZZA
I love pizza!
"Let's go shopping!"
New York is famous for its music – especially hip-hop, rock and jazz.
DINER
BREAKFAST LUNCH DINNER
DINER
餐厅
药店 PHARMACY
New York's famous yellow taxis are a great way to get around the city.
People from all over the world have settled in New York, and around 800 languages are spoken here.
泡泡茶
面条
TAXI
TAXI
DELICATESSEN
Statue of Liberty
Brooklyn Bridge
Manhattan Bridge
STOP
FRANKLIN AV
COFFEE
RECORDS

Broadway is New York's famous theatre district. Lots of incredible musicals and plays are performed here every night.
Times Square
COMING SOON
FLY
NEW
"How do I get to Central Park?"
"Taxi!"
Traffic light
American Museum of Natural History
The New York Public Library holds around 50 million books!
Central Park Zoo
Central Park
Built in 1931, the 102-storey Empire State Building was the tallest building in the world until 1970.
Chrysler Building
The Metropolitan Museum of Art, also called 'The Met', is the largest art museum in the Americas.
Skyscraper
THE SOLOMON R. GUGGENHEIM MUSEUM
"I feel like an ant!"
ONE WAY
Manhattan is an island, surrounded by the Hudson, East and Harlem rivers.
Solomon R. Guggenheim Museum (modern art museum)
New York is split into five boroughs: Queens, The Bronx, Brooklyn, Manhattan and Staten Island.
Williamsburg Bridge
BAR
COMICS
The NYC Subway opened in 1904. It runs all day every day and has a route length of 399 kilometres.
9

LONDON
About nine million people live in London, the capital of England. Although the main language spoken in England is English, there are an incredible 300 languages spoken in London, making it one of the most linguistically diverse cities in the world!
Notting Hill Carnival takes place every summer. This celebration of Caribbean culture has been running since 1966.
Royal Albert Hall
Big Ben
Buckingham Palace
There is a delicious and diverse food scene, with food available from every corner of the world.
Hungerford Bridge and Golden Jubilee Bridges
telephone box
TELEPHONE
bus stop
London Eye
Tea Rooms
FISH & CHIPS
Restaurant
The British drink up to 165 million cups of tea a day!
10

Amazingly, London has so many trees it is officially recognised as a forest!
duck
picnic
fox
London has a rich creative scene. It's home to three of the top ten museums and galleries in the world, and has over 300 live music venues.
The National Gallery
Royal Opera House
Tate Modern (art gallery)
Southbank Centre
"Hello!"
bicycle
taxi
station
bus
"Which way is the ticket office?"
The metro system in London is called 'the tube'. This underground network is the oldest in the world and today has over 270 stations.
train
rat

PARIS
Paris is the capital of France. It is sometimes referred to as 'the city of light', but this is not only because of its dazzling street lamps and neon signs – Paris is full of wonderful culture and history that 'illuminates' the mind!
Sacré-Coeur Basilica
"Au revoir!" ("Goodbye!")
voiture (car)
oiseau (bird)
Arc de Triomphe
Historically, Paris was one of the most influential cities in the world for art. Today, you can still see works of the great masters including Picasso, Monet, Renoir and Dalí, as well as some fantastic modern art.
The Louvre
The River Seine flows through Paris, and has an incredible 37 bridges built along its route. One of the most famous is referred to as Pont des Artes or 'Love Lock Bridge', as many happy couples have declared their love for one another by attaching a lock to the bridge.
Musée d'Orsay
bateau (boat)
The Eiffel Tower
arbre (tree)
Home to over 500 parks and gardens, Paris is one of the greenest cities in Europe.
Pont d'Iéna
12

One of the most wonderful things about Paris is all of the delicious French pastries on offer. You can find them in many patisseries.

The bouquinistes of Paris set up their stalls along the River Seine. Selling beautiful antique and second-hand books, these booksellers have been trading for over 500 years!

Giradabo
(ferris wheel)
Throughout the year, every neighbourhood hosts a Festa Major. Each street festival has its own traditions, with parades, music, dancing and food.
Parque Güell (ES)
Parc Güell (CA)
(Park Güell)
fútbol (ES)
futbol (CA)
(football)
"¡Bailemos!" (ES)
"¡Ballem!" (CA)
("Let's dance!")
música
(music)
Casa Milà (a famous building designed by Antoni Gaudí)
National Art Museum of Catalonia
Las Ramblas (ES)
Les Rambles (CA)
"¡Disculpe!" (ES),
"¡Perdoni!" (CA)
("Excuse me!")
teleférico (ES)
telefèric (CA)
(cable cars)
14

BARCELONA

Barcelona sits on the Mediterranean coast of Spain. This sunny city is home to over three million people and receives over 15 million visitors from around the world every year. There are two official languages spoken in Barcelona – Spanish (ES) and Catalan (CA).

"Adios" (ES)
"Adéu" (CA)
("Goodbye")

With lots of sunshine and an average of only 55 days of rain a year, it's no surprise that nearly half of all journeys in Barcelona are made on foot or by bike.

Antoni Gaudí designed many buildings in Barcelona, including the Sagrada Família. Construction of the Basilica began in 1882 and, once it is complete, it will be the tallest church building in the world at 172 metres high.

pasear (ES), passejar (CA)
(to stroll)

Catedral de Barcelona

Arco de Triunfo (ES)
Arc de Triomf (CA)

bicicleta
(bicycle)

"Te amo." (ES)
"T'estimo." (CA)
("I love you.")

The markets of Barcelona offer mouth-watering delights. Many people enjoy sharing tapas – different small dishes – while talking into the night.

"Gracias" (ES)
"Gràcies" (CA)
("Thank you")

autobús
(bus)

"Hola"
("Hello")

Barceloneta Beach

helado (ES)
gelat (CA)
(ice cream)

15

AMSTERDAM
"Ik hou van pannenkoeken!" ("I love pancakes!")
Amsterdam is the capital of the Netherlands and home to around 900,000 people. The primary language spoken here is Dutch. The land the city is built on is wet and soft. To stop buildings from sinking, they were constructed on top of thousands of wooden poles driven deep into harder ground.
Sometimes called 'the Venice of the North', Amsterdam has over 100 kilometres of canals. Built in the 17th century, they were dug out entirely by hand.
Amsterdam Centraal
"Hallo" ("Hello")
Anne Frank House
Royal Palace
Dam Square
gracht (canal)
Floating Flower Market
The canals make boating around the city a fun and convenient way to get around.
Stedelijk Museum (modern art museum)
Van Gogh Museum
Amsterdam
Rijksmuseum (art gallery)
16

Java-eiland
(Java Island)
veerboot
(ferry)
auto
(car)
Roughly 4,000 wild parakeets have made Amsterdam their home.
NEMO Science Museum
Scheepvaartmuseum
(maritime museum)
windmolen
(windmill)
Cycling is popular in Amsterdam and there are nearly as many bikes in the city as people!
Rembrandt House Museum
vogels
(birds)
leeuw
(lion)
tulpen
(tulips)
giraffe
(giraffe)
"Tot ziens"
("Goodbye")
zebra
(zebra)
Artis
(zoo and garden)
neushoorn
(rhinoceros)
Bitterballen –
deep-fried
meatballs
"Bedankt!"
("Thank you!")
Amsterdam has around 1,200 bridges.
"Lekker!"
("Delicious!")
Amsterdam is famous for its tulips. During April's Tulip Festival, the city is covered in their colourful blooms!

17

Hauptbahnhof (main train station)
"Fahrkarten, bitte!" ("Tickets, please!")
River Spree
fledermaus (bat, or literally 'fluttering mouse')
hund (dog)
vogel (bird)
Reichstag (government office)
Brandenburg Gate
GEMÜSE KEBAP
Berlin Victory Column
blumen (flowers)
baum (tree)
eichhörnchen (squirrel)
pflaumenkuchen mit streuseln (plum crumble cake)
wurst (sausage)
"Ich liebe dich" ("I love you")
"Danke!" ("Thank you!")
wildschwein (wild boar)
Founded in 1844, Berlin Zoological Garden is the oldest zoo in Germany. It is also the most visited in Europe and considered to have the largest number of animals in the world. Berlin has local wildlife, too!
waschbär (raccoon)
katze (cat)
"Los geht's!" ("let's go!")
picknick (picnic)
18

BERLIN
Over four million people live in the German-speaking city of Berlin, the largest city in Germany. After the Second World War, Germany was split in two. In 1990, the country reunited, and Berlin became the capital of Germany again. Today you can experience its history on every street corner.
turmfalke (tower kestrel)
Berlin Fernsehturm (Berlin TV Tower)
"Tschüss!" ("Bye!")
FRIEDEN
From 1949 to 1990, the city was divided into East and West Berlin, with a wall separating them. Most of the wall was torn down when the city was reunited, but one remaining part forms the East Side Gallery – the largest open-air museum in the world.
Bode-Museum
FALAFEL
Berlin Cathedral
Museum Island (a UNESCO World Heritage Site with five museums)
taube (pigeon)
ampel (traffic light)
LIEBE
U-Bahn (train system)
U1
Oberbaumbrücke (Oberbaum Bridge)
auto (car)
fahrrad (bike)
DÖNER
"Hallo!" ("Hello!")
Some of Berlin's most famous dishes – including the döner kebab – were introduced by Arab and Turkish immigrants who brought their culinary traditions to the city.
boot (boat)
ente (duck)
19

Pál-völgyi
(cave)
"Szeretlek!"
("I love you!")
Pinball Museum
Margaret
Island
"Helló!"
("Hello!")
Matthias
Church
Stretching for 2,850 kilometres, the Danube is the second longest river in Europe. It begins in Germany and passes through ten countries before flowing into the Black Sea.
Fisherman's
Bastion
(fortress)
Somlói galuska is a delicious pudding consisting of layers of sponge, cream and chocolate sauce.
Buda Castle
Built in 1849, the 375-metre-long Széchenyi Chain Bridge spans the Danube to connect Buda and Pest.
funicular
"Viszlát!"
("Bye!")
20

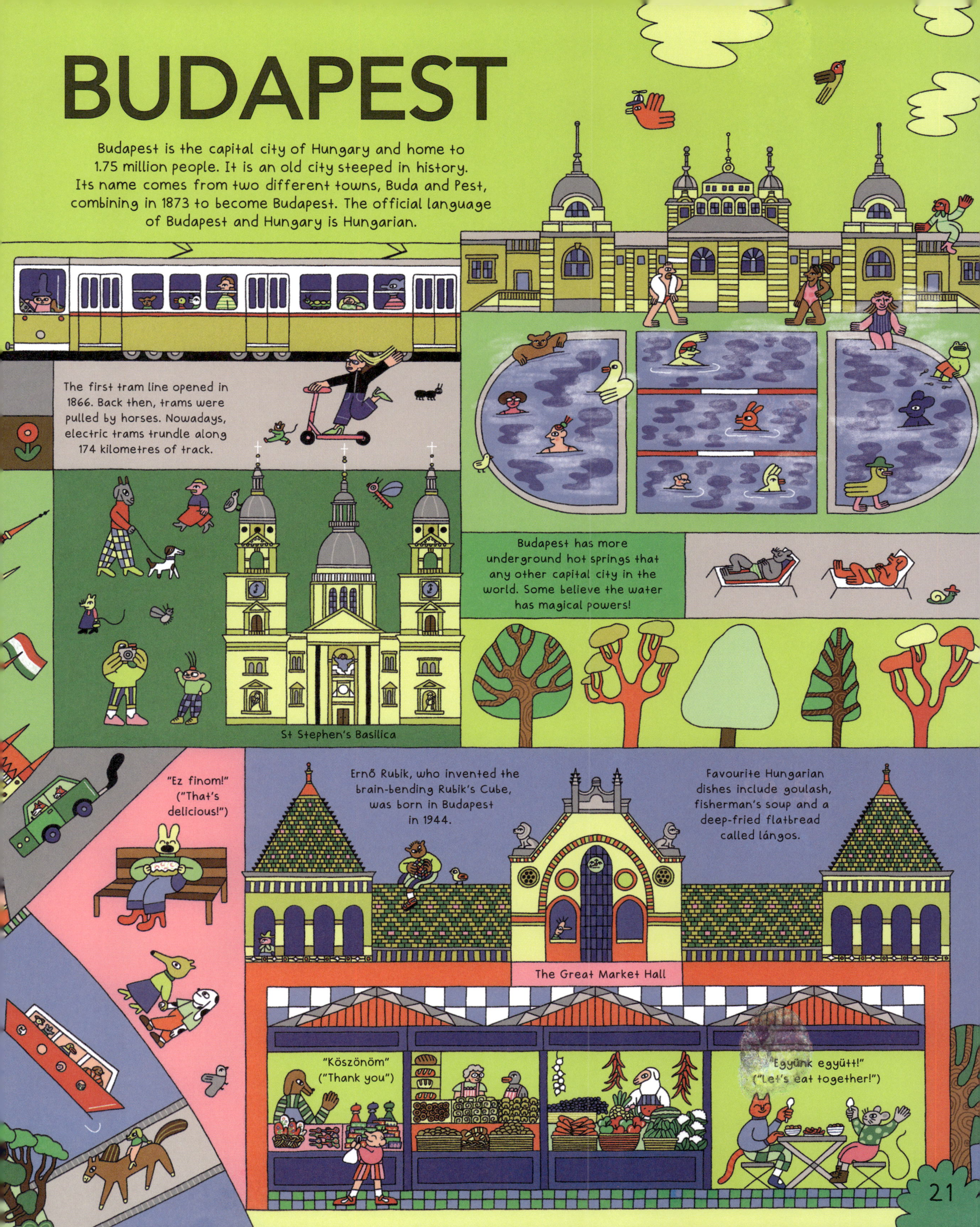

BUDAPEST
Budapest is the capital city of Hungary and home to 1.75 million people. It is an old city steeped in history. Its name comes from two different towns, Buda and Pest, combining in 1873 to become Budapest. The official language of Budapest and Hungary is Hungarian.
The first tram line opened in 1866. Back then, trams were pulled by horses. Nowadays, electric trams trundle along 174 kilometres of track.
Budapest has more underground hot springs that any other capital city in the world. Some believe the water has magical powers!
St Stephen's Basilica
"Ez finom!" ("That's delicious!")
Ernő Rubik, who invented the brain-bending Rubik's Cube, was born in Budapest in 1944.
Favourite Hungarian dishes include goulash, fisherman's soup and a deep-fried flatbread called lángos.
The Great Market Hall
"Köszönöm" ("Thank you")
"Együnk együtt!" ("Let's eat together!")

# ROME

Founded around 753 BCE, Rome is an ancient city and was once the centre of the Roman Empire. Each year, around nine million tourists visit the capital of Italy to explore its ruins, experience its rich culture of food and fashion, and speak Italian with the locals.



Rome contains Vatican City, the world's smallest independent nation state. This tiny country is only 0.44 square kilometres and has a population of around 450.

Rome has around 2,000 fountains – more than any other city in the world.

Rome is home to thousands of stray cats, which are protected by law and allowed to live freely throughout the city.

maritozzi – light brioche buns filled with cream

"Ciao!"
("Hello!")
Galleria Borghese
(art gallery)
scultura
(sculpture)
PIAZZA
CAFFETTERIA BAR RISTORANTE
Carbonara – pasta made with pork, black pepper, hard cheese and eggs (not cream!)
Spanish Steps
Piazza Navona
Every day, tourists drop around €3,000 into the Trevi Fountain.
Capuchin Crypt
GELATI DRINKS BIBITE
mercato
(market)
ponte
(bridge)
Roman Forum
(open-air museum)
The Colosseum is one of the most famous ruins in the world.
Palatine Hill

ISTANBUL

Istanbul has a long, rich history. Once the capital of the Byzantine and Ottoman Empires, it's now the largest city in Turkey. It's also the only city to straddle two continents: Europe and Asia. The main language spoken here is Turkish.

"Bu halıyı beğendim" ("I like this carpet")

Grand Bazaar

"Merhaba" ("Hello")

"Açım" ("I'm hungry")

"Teşekkür ederim" ("Thank you")

Topkapı Palace

The name Istanbul comes from the Greek phrase 'stinpolis', meaning 'to the city'. Before this, it was known as Byzantium, then New Rome, and later Constantinople. In 1930 it was renamed Istanbul.

kedi (cat)

Hagia Sophia

"Bu lezzetli" ("That's delicious!")

BALIK RESTORANI

The Blue Mosque

24

With around 15 million tourists visiting every year, Istanbul is one of the most popular cities in the world.
Galata Tower
Bosphorus Bridge
Maiden's Tower
Hamam (Turkish bath)
baklava – sweet and tasty pastry
PASTANE
"Seni seviyorum!" ("I love you!")
BAKKAL
Turkish delight – a jellied sweet delicacy often flavoured with rosewater, orange or lemon
Tea is drunk regularly when socialising. Turkish people each drink an average of 3 kilograms of tea per year – more than any other country in the world!
"Türk lokumunu seviyorum!" ("I love Turkish delight!")
çay bahçesi
simit – circle-shaped bread covered with sesame seeds
tekne (boat)
"Hoşça kal" ("Goodbye")
25

Gyeongbokgung
"안녕하세요"
annyeong-haseyo
("Hello")
Amongst the high-rises and skyscrapers lies Bukchon Hanok Village. It has 900 hanoks – traditional Korean houses with wooden frames and tiled roofs that have been preserved for over 600 years.
In Korean, karaoke is called 'norae-bang' which means 'song room'. There are many karaoke bars in Seoul where you can sing your heart out!
"인삼차 한잔 드릴까요?"
insam-cha hanjan deurilkkayo?
("May I have some ginseng tea?")
Cafe culture is huge in Seoul. There are even cafes with resident cats that customers can pet while enjoying a drink!
노래방
카페
OPEN
Seoul Museum of Art
Sungnyemun Gate
N Seoul Tower
Namsan Park
"안녕히 가세요"
annyeonghi gaseyo
("Goodbye")
Parc1
63 Building
Seoul has over 30 bridges spanning the Han River.
Banpo Bridge and Rainbow Fountain
ARCADE
26

SEOUL

Founded in the 18th century BCE, the capital city of South Korea is now home to around ten million people. This gleaming city is a major centre of science and technology, and it also boasts five UNESCO World Heritage Sites.

Seoul boasts five palaces. Changdeokgung, built in 1395 BCE, is the oldest.

hanbok – traditional Korean clothing

"나는 김치를 사랑해요!"
naneun gimchireul saranghaeyo
("I love kimchi!")

Dongdaemun Design Plaza

Korean barbecue (known as gogi-gui or 한국식 바베큐) is a popular Korean cuisine, where diners can grill their own meat at the table.

고기집

"맛있어요!"
masi-sseo-yo
("That's delicious!")

Metro system

"날씨가 참 좋네요!"
nalssiga cham johneyo
("The weather is lovely!")

Seoul Forest Park

Lotte World

"같이 먹자!"
gat-i meogja
("Let's eat together!")

GANG NAM STYLE

"감사합니다"
gamsahamnida
("Thank you")

Seokchon Lake

"사랑해요!"
saranghaeyo
("I love you!")

KARAOKE
カラオケ
カフェ
HOTEL
¥200
ネットカフェ
カラオケ
¥200
焼き肉
24時間
OKONOMIYAKI
お好み焼き
"こんにちは"
"konnichiwa"
("hello")
はな
hana
(flower)
Every spring, Tokyo is covered in beautiful pink and white blossom called 'sakura'. It is traditional to have a picnic under the blossom during the season.
Lots of wild animals live in harmony with people in this busy city.
Meiji Jingu Shrine
たぬき
tanuki
(Japanese racoon dog)
ARCADE
"かっこいい!"
"kakkoii!"
("Cool!")
HOCKEY
Nearly every district has a 'sento' (bathhouse). It is a big part of Japanese culture.
渋谷
ばす
basu
(bus)
おいしい
ヨーグルト
BOOK
The Shibuya Crossing is one of the busiest pedestrian crossings in the world. More than 2,000 people cross the seven streets every time the lights turn green!
くるま
kuruma
(car)
sushi – vinegared rice rolled with ingredients such as seafood or vegetables
"おいしい!"
"Oishii!"
("Yum!")
Gotokuji Temple
(Lucky Cat Temple)
かわいい
kawaī
(cute)
28

TOKYO
Far from the small fishing village it once was, the capital of Japan is now home to 37 million people – the largest population of any city in the world. With both neon-lit skyscrapers and ancient temples, Tokyo has an incredible mix of sights to see.
"ありがとう!"
"Arigatou!"
("Thank you!")
Senso-ji temple
たい焼き
taiyaki – a fish-shaped pastry, often filled with sweetened red bean paste
¥200
There are over 4,000 shrines and temples in Tokyo. Shinto and Buddhism are Japan's two major religions. Shinto worshippers attend shrines, while Buddhists attend temples.
Tokyo Station
Tokyo Skytree
きっぷ
kippu
(ticket)
3↑ →↑4
出口
でんしゃ
densha
(train)
The Shinkansen is also called the Japanese Bullet Train. It's one of the fastest trains in the world, capable of travelling 320 kilometres per hour!
Sumida River
ramen – a noodle soup, often served with pork, nori (seaweed) and a boiled egg
ラーメン
Tokyo Tower
き
ki
(tree)
Rainbow Bridge

# GOODBYE!

Our world is full of wonderful, diverse places –
bright cities, colourful markets, wide oceans and
tall mountains. We've travelled to just 12 incredible
cities, but there is so much more to discover.

Every place is home to people who speak different
languages, tell unique stories and share special
traditions. Every word you learn helps you connect
with someone and understand their culture.

Let's keep exploring, learning and celebrating the
voices that make up our big, brilliant world.

Bye!
See ya!
Arrivederci!
Ciao!
Viszontlátásra!
Viszlát!
じゃあね
(Jā ne)
さようなら
(Sayōnara)
Adéu!
A reveure!
Adiós!
Hasta luego!

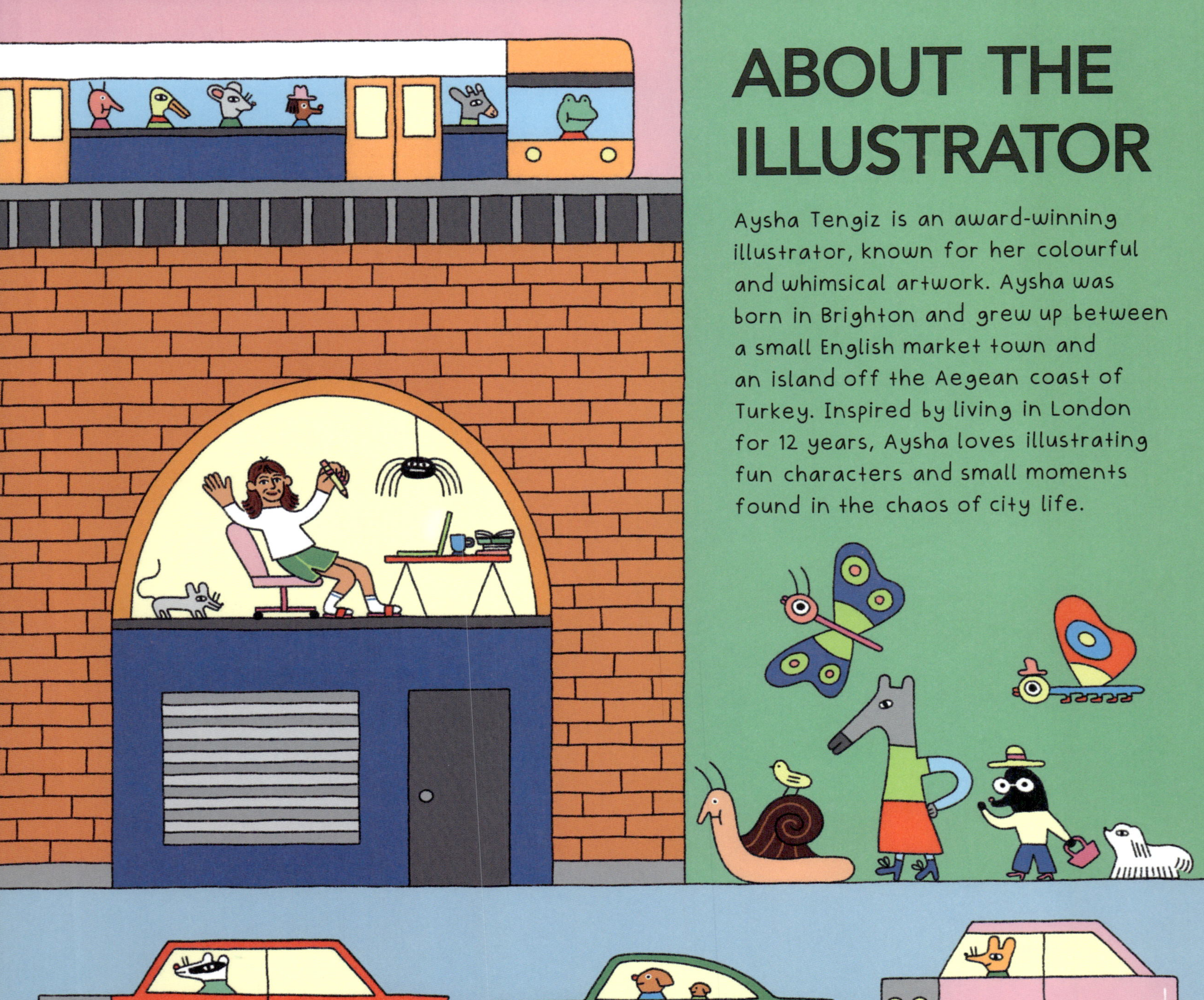

# ABOUT THE ILLUSTRATOR

Aysha Tengiz is an award-winning illustrator, known for her colourful and whimsical artwork. Aysha was born in Brighton and grew up between a small English market town and an island off the Aegean coast of Turkey. Inspired by living in London for 12 years, Aysha loves illustrating fun characters and small moments found in the chaos of city life.

BIG PICTURE PRESS

First published in the UK in 2026
by Big Picture Press,
an imprint of Bonnier Books UK
5th Floor, HYLO,
105 Bunhill Row,
London, EC1Y 8LZ

The authorised representative in the EEA
is Bonnier Books UK (Ireland) Limited.
Registered office address:
Block B, The Crescent Building
Northwood, Santry
Dublin 9, D09 C6X8, Ireland

compliance@bonnierbooks.ie
www.bonnierbooks.co.uk

Illustration copyright © 2026
by Aysha Tengiz
Text and design copyright © 2026
by Big Picture Press

10 9 8 7 6 5 4 3 2 1

All rights reserved
ISBN 978-1-83587-095-2

This book was typeset in the
illustrator's own typeface and Avenir.

The illustrations were created digitally.

Written by Matt Ralphs and Lisa Davis
Designed by Winsome d'Abreu
Edited by Josephine Southon
Sensitivity read by Nozomi Tolworthy
Production by Nick Read

Printed in China